# RUNNING OUT OF DRUGS

# ROYA JOYA

Published in the United States

First Edition

Imprint: Independently published

Cover Design: Vanessa Mendozzi

Book Design: Ashley Santoro

ISBN: 9798444329085

# Table of Contents

I would like to dedicate this book to my parents, whose self-proclamation as standup comedians I inherited, and to my brother, who taught me to find humor in the worst and best of times.

# Preface

I would like to begin by stating that I love the pharmacy profession, especially retail pharmacy. My time in retail has been filled with amazing memories, opportunities, and people. I wanted to shed light on the humor of retail pharmacy and how society has developed over time.

I wrote this book for all of the underappreciated healthcare providers. To the esteemed doctors who are demeaned by patients who can't tell right from left. To the technicians who are treated like they are cashiers. For the people who want to slam their head against a wall as they watch the intelligence among our society decline at a rapid rate—this is for you.

And to the early healthcare professionals who appear too young to be taken seriously, your contributions matter.

Finally, any story or recounting that may raise eyebrows beyond general stupidity was investigated further and passed along to the appropriate party. I never hesitate to contact authorities whether it's the medical board, pharmacy board, Division of Child and Family Services (DCFS), or police when the situation calls. Wherever danger is found or suspected, it was and will be reported. I am not in the business of gambling with lives.

# Part One:
# The Process

# Pizza Hut

WE ARE NOT A PIZZA HUT. I repeat, we are NOT a Pizza Hut. On a daily basis, we find visitors surprised to learn that the pharmacy is not, in fact, a fast-food chain with pre-made food that is ready in the six minutes one spends waiting in line.

There is no hot and ready pizza to pick up without ordering. If you do not sign up for an auto refill program, and do not call your medications in, why would your medication be ready for you? My telepathic powers are not strong enough to know when to fill everyone's medications each and every day. If you need a medication, call it in ahead of time. Do not waste my or my staff's time waiting and staring at us.

Do not ask the staff to "slap a label" on a box. If that was our only duty, then the world should be very concerned about our overpaid profession. You would be amazed by the number of people who approach the counter with a prescription and preface with, "It's just a cream so you can just slap a label on it." No sir, I cannot "slap a label" on anything. Unfortunately, the process of preparing medication begins with the prescription intake, then data entry into the computer system, which will print a nifty label that most people still refuse to read. Upon the receipt of the label, a technician scours the perpetually unorganized alphabetic shelves until they find the correct medication (most likely in the wrong location, under the wrong name, next to a package that looks just like it). The technician then takes the cream box and scans it to produce a label to "slap on" the box and send to the all-purpose pharmacist to check. Keep in mind there are some pharmacists who end up checking seven hundred to nine hundred prescriptions in a retail setting every day. This means pharmacists check those medications while counseling patients with insane needs and carrying on inane conversation to appease the lonely population that comes to the pharmacy looking for friends. "Slapping a label" is quite a process of its own.

Back to Pizza Hut—there is no refund for a half-eaten pizza, and you don't get to choose what brand of cheese they put on your pizza. So why would it be reasonable to return medication you've taken for a week and then decided nope, you don't like it? Or what about people who swear up and down that they can only take one brand of a specific medication? Okay, fine, it is possible that there are some differences between brands. But jeez, people, do you really know better than your doctor?

Also, if you can order a pizza and remember to pick it up, then why can't you remember to pick up medications? In all honesty, I would like to say that pizza is the most important thing in the world (to me at least), but medication is probably a *smidgen* more important. So why not pick it up? YOU call the pharmacy and order it, YOU demand a time you want it, and YOU don't pick it up. On average at a high-traffic pharmacy, ten prescriptions are returned to stock every day. Consider that this percentage equates to roughly seventy forgotten prescriptions a week. Prescriptions are returned to the shelf after twelve days of being filled. So, in almost two weeks you couldn't find time to pick it up?

Pizza, on the other hand, is picked up within twenty minutes of ordering it . . . strange where all our priorities are these days.

Lastly, it is amazing how people will complain about having to wait at the pharmacy because their medications were put back on the shelf. Well geniuses of America, if you find time to visit us in the twelve days following your prescription pickup request, you won't have to wait an *unreasonable* amount of time. Speaking of unreasonable waits, when was it more socially acceptable to camp outside of Best Buy on Black Friday than to wait in the pharmacy for the outrageous TWENTY minutes during rush hour? Step back. Think. Learn. Do better next time.

END RANT. . . . Better yet, begin the next rant.

# The Process

## What Does a Pharmacist Do?

Society's impression of a pharmacist seems to be someone who "slaps a label" (oh, my favorite phrase!) on a box and throws some pills into a bottle. As time goes on, more and more people have gone from being patients at a pharmacy to acting as its customers—demanding quicker service and getting outraged by the level of care we try to offer. However, I am here to set the record straight. We do NOT just throw pills in a bottle. Again, if we did, you should be very concerned with our rather steep salary for a mindless task, no?

A pharmacist is turned to as a therapist, a problem solver, a detective, an insurance quoter, an immunizer, a sympathizer, a housekeeper, a counselor, an exterminator, a referral service, a leadership coach, a first responder, a security guard, a shelf stocker, a store navigator, and basically Google. If you consider our many titles and faces, then you'd know our salaries are no match for society's expectations.

People constantly call me asking for medical advice because it is FREE. Some say they trust us more; some say they believe in our abilities; some say that we are their longest connection to medicine. While flattering or maybe sad, at the end of the day, we know we are just more accessible and cheaper than other medical professionals. To those people who take advantage of that, kudos to you for figuring it out. To those who wrongfully turn to healthcare professionals demanding inappropriate assistance, I'm sorry you're too ignorant to realize that.

## Things I Cannot Fix in RETAIL Pharmacy Settings:

1. Fresh gunshot wound—I cannot remove a bullet in a non-sterile environment and pack the wound for you because it was "just an accident," and you don't want to pay an emergency room fee. Enjoy your amputation because that wound won't survive without proper medical attention.

2. Car malfunctions—I'm not quite sure why you'd come into a pharmacy and ask us what is wrong with your car if there's a gas station across the street. However, no sir—I am not that kind of doctor. I know nothing about cars.

3. Objects retained anally—I try not to judge people and their activities, but when you walk into my store

to tell me you have a small object stuck in your rectum and need help . . . what did you really think I was going to do? Have you undress in the waiting room (a.k.a. aisle twenty-three) and remove the object for you? Nope, not that kind of doctor either.

4. Marital problems—I am not legally allowed to refuse the sale of a medication to a man because his wife "says so." Curious? Yes, a wife entered the pharmacy and demanded we no longer fill and dispense her husband's erectile dysfunction medications because she was seeing someone else and didn't want to keep "dealing with him." When we explained that the man has a right to his prescriptions, she confronted us with the, "Well, I say it needs to stop and it better before I report you." For . . . what exactly?

5. Abortions—touchy subject for many these days, but in this regard, we are unable to do anything in this matter. A patient who reaches out seeking the morning-after pill is warned about the consequences and how the medication is to be used. However, to the woman who called four months pregnant asking how to use the tablet to "resolve this issue"—no ma'am. You are not a candidate for this medication, and you are aware of that fact. You are not a candidate for any sort of abortive medication, and you are seeking medical assistance through the wrong channel. I hope you followed our advice and contacted the proper healthcare advisors because, again, no ma'am.

These examples are just a few of the subjects that

come to mind when I think of tasks I cannot complete. Now, let's discuss the essence of a job in a retail pharmacy. The process itself. The main attraction.

## Process of a Prescription:

1. Prescription is obtained from a provider. That is, if you went to the doctor and physically got a paper copy of the prescription. What if you need a refill on a script you already have and you are waiting for the doctor to send it in? See Factor #2.

> i.   Let's say it's a new script being faxed over to the pharmacy in this super techy world we live in. Ninety-nine percent of people always say, "HIS NURSE SENT IT OVER WHEN I WAS THERE." No, they did not. See as the process goes, the doctor has to sign off on the prescriptions, which some providers do in bulk review rather than one script per person.

2. Prescription is delivered to the pharmacy.

> ii.   You're waiting for a refill on a previous prescription. Most of these requests are processed only once per day. They aren't handled continuously because, again, the provider has to sign off on the request and, if you've been to see a doctor lately, you know they don't sit behind a computer

all day waiting to sign your prescriptions. They see patients, write reports and fill out charts, and then get around to the work for the patients they didn't see that day. So, instead of getting mad at the pharmacy for not having the prescription or the doctor for not doing their job, think about how your doctor has examined about twenty people, wrote twenty reports, and is trying to add you onto his or her plans behind the hundreds of other requests he or she must complete in one day. As for the small-town pharmacy, you're one of roughly two hundred to three hundred people they've seen that day.

*Side note: Contrary to popular belief, we cannot just "give you a couple tablets" while you wait. I know how inconvenient it is that we can't just loan you some Oxycodone in good faith because of drug abusers, but so goes life. . . .*

3. Prescription is entered at the pharmacy.

This filling process entails a technician or pharmacist typing in the proper information and directions under the patient's profile. Simple enough until there are eighteen phone calls, six people in line, twelve other scripts to type, and only two people taming the madhouse that is a pharmacy because Betty Sue is on her lunch break. In this case, it won't be a five-minute wait anymore. When you see the struggle is upon the pharmacy and the dark clouds are closing in, don't expect to wait your normal 10-15 minutes. Some pharmacies won't tell you the truth, but I sure will.

4. Entered prescription is checked by the Pharmacist.

    iii.    Ah, my favorite part. The pre-check to the final check of all the checks. Click three buttons to confirm it's good to go and boom! The prescription is ready to print and fill! Oh wait, I hope it was for the right person. Just press the buttons as quickly as possible because Karen has to go pick up her kid from soccer practice, and this prescription from four months ago is an emergency. NO. The answer is NO. I REFUSE to push through this process. I refuse to allow the patients or technicians rush me through verification. No. THIS is how you end up in a hospital with an ugly rash across your left cheek. This is how people die. This five-minute step should take as long as it needs to, and everyone should be A-OK with it because it saves lives. So, sit back, shut your pie-hole, and allow the person who spent eight years in professional school decide if the medication is entered correctly.

5. Prescription is filled by a technician.

> After verification, the prescription prints out *(hope there's not a paper jam again!)*, and the technicians are able to locate the drug *(unless it's on back order with the other 2,358 medications)* and fill the medication. If it's a narcotic medication, it is counted twice by hand *(hope it's less than 120 so they count fast, otherwise we could be here all night!)*. Then the medication bottle and label are handed down to the pharmacist. "Slapping a label" on it roughly fifteen minutes into the process isn't what the patient expected, right?

6. Filled Prescription is checked by pharmacist

> iv. The *crème de la crème* of the process. Finally, I get to see if the last twenty-five minutes were worth it. I make sure the correct item is in the bottle and in the correct quantity. Oh, how I love donating a portion of my memory to what the tablets should look like. Photographic memory serves me well during this phase.

7. Prescription is placed on the shelf for pickup.

> v. Seventy-two. That's how many bins there are to place prescriptions in by alphabetical order. But John Jr. has been waiting in the store, and his prescription could be

anywhere. It could be waiting next to the pharmacist station to be put up, it could already be in the bin. It could be in the waiter basket. Wait, was it refrigerated? The options are endless. The new technician is sweating bullets as John Jr. burns a hole in the back of her head. She frantically searches the pharmacy. John Jr. bin number twenty-two, where are you? Left. Right. Up. Down. Nowhere to be found. Finally, she asks for help from her fellow tech-mates, and now John Jr. is fed up with the way business is being conducted. He just dropped the script off and waited thirty minutes, but in the homestretch, the bag went on vacation to Aruba and was abducted. Bad joke. Too soon? ALAS! John Jr. bin twenty-two was placed in thirty-two because all numbers look alike when you're overwhelmed.

Seems simple enough right? Eh . . . depends on the day. Consider if each step took five minutes. It takes five minutes to make my favorite microwave mac 'n' cheese, so I guess I'll dedicate five minutes to making sure a life isn't lost. Five minutes per step, seven steps—that's up to thirty-five minutes, right? Then why is it people's eyes get big when we say it'll be a fifteen-to-twenty-minute wait? Concerned about your well-being or your ability to beat your kids home to eat the last Choco Taco in the freezer? If waiting at the pharmacy for more than twenty minutes for one prescription is the worst part of your day, perhaps your day wasn't so bad after all.

# Insurance Debacle

KNOW YOUR INSURANCE PLANS.
I cannot stress this enough so repeat after me:

I WILL KNOW MY INSURANCE PLAN.

I WILL KNOW MY INSURANCE PLAN.

I WILL KNOW MY INSURANCE PLAN.

I WILL KNOW MY INSURANCE PLAN.

When you sign up for insurance, you choose from a variety of plans. Some are better than others, which means you read to find out which plan is better. You try to see what the difference is among them. So how, HOW is it possible that you do not know what your plans entail? Not only at sign-up, but also when you receive the cards in the mail? You will get a formulary sheet and an explanation of benefits. Now, wouldn't it make sense to keep these papers while they are relevant? Nope. Just toss them like last night's dinner. Actually, you probably kept last night's leftovers.

More than half of the people we see daily have no idea what their insurance plan entails. They don't know what their copays are, if they have deductibles (some don't even know what deductible is), or what their prescription insurance cards look like.

## Common Misconceptions Debunked:

1. NO, we cannot search your insurance by your name.

2. NO, we do not have a running list of every single patient's insurance information as it changes.

3. NO, God does not telepathically send me your information when you tell me you have Blue Cross Blue Shield insurance.

4. NO, the pharmacy does not control the prices of your medications.

    a. *Now this is quite unfortunate. Whether you annoy me or not, you have to pay the same price. Imagine if we could change the prices depending on how we felt. Most of the population would pay ten times more than they should because of their terrible attitudes.*

5. NO, pharmacies cannot fill a prescription in under one minute.

    a. We do NOT just "put some tablets in a bottle" and if we did, you should be very afraid. You are welcome to take the time to look at your medications and make sure they match the prescriptions written for you. You are welcome for keeping you alive.

## Scenario:

*patient enters the pharmacy to pick up a prescription*

**Pharmacist:** "That will be 178 dollars."

**Patient:** *[mini heart attack]* "WHAT? WHY?"

**Pharmacist:** "Your deductible resets at the beginning of the year, and it has not been met yet."

**Patient:** "Deductible? I don't have a deductible. I don't even know what a deductible is."

**Pharmacist:** *[so . . . you don't know what it is but you are SURE you don't have one? Interesting]*

*explains the meaning of deductible*

"If you would like to call your insurance company to discuss your plan with them before picking up your medication, we can hold it here for you"

**Patient:** "Well, can you give me the medication, and then I will call the insurance afterwards?"

**Pharmacist:** "Sure, that will be 178 dollars."

**Patient:** "WHAT? Why can't I just get it at the normal copay price until they fix it?"

**Pharmacist:** [*what I'd like to say is, "because we are* NOT *in the business of giving away medications for free," but in reality, we know that patients cannot handle the truth*]

"You have to spend three-hundred dollars out of pocket before your copay kicks in"

**Patient:** "Oh. They told me I had to pay cash out of pocket; I just thought I got to choose when."

**Pharmacist:** [*FACEPALM*]

Now, in situations like this, you have to think to yourself: After twenty minutes of back and forth where you didn't know what a deductible was and you swore you didn't have one, all of the sudden you have one? You have not only wasted a ton of your own time; you've also, more importantly, wasted mine. I say "more importantly" because pharmacists are only important to themselves, so I have to look out for number one.

## Patient Tips:

1. Call your insurance company (the number on the back of the card) if you ever have any questions. They can always assist you so you don't have to wait inside of a high-traffic pharmacy like sardines.

2. The pharmacy will refuse to help you when you don't know what is going on but insist you do. We know the difference between intelligent people and unaware patients. I promise, I know when you're bullshitting.

# Doctor's Problems

There are a whole host of issues that are the DOCTOR'S PROBLEM, NOT the pharmacy's. We don't tell you to call the doctor because we think it would be fun to watch you sit on hold listening to elevator music for eighteen minutes.

## What a Pharmacy Cannot Do:

1. The pharmacy cannot renew your prescription. No matter how much you beg and plead, it legally cannot happen so don't waste either of our times.

2. The pharmacy cannot diagnose and give you prescription medications. There are plenty of instances where we can help you find something over the counter for a cold or mild illness, but some people have gone far beyond our scope of practice.

*patient limps towards the pharmacy; appears to be lost in the desert*

**Patient:** "Hi, where can I find your gauze, bandages, and scar cream?"

**Pharmacist**: "Let me show you."

*walks over to first aid aisle*

"Now, what are you using this for—maybe I can help a little better."

**Patient**: "I have a gunshot wound, so I need to pack it to stop the bleeding because I took the bullet out, and I don't want to have another scar."

**Pharmacist**: *[ . . . truly stunned. Is this real life? You didn't call 911, go to an ER, or even try to see an Urgent Care? You came to the pharmacy? What?]*

"I believe you should go to the ER so they can take a look at that for you. The wound could get infected and lead to other health problems."

**Patient**: "No, it's okay, I did this last time, too."

Who am I to argue with this logic? Clearly, this patient is experienced in the art of gunshot wound recovery. Which brings about my next question. . . . How many times has this happened? Was it an accident? Is there a perpetrator on the loose? Should I carry mace on my way out? Do I really think my mace would suffice against a gun? I guess it's better than the fork I have in my bag from lunch?

# Too Young for Health Care

Too often I see college students come to the pharmacy for antidepressants, stimulants, or other expensive medications that they will pay for in cash.

Public Service Announcement: Parents, do not insure your children if they are too dumb/young/naive to know how to use insurance cards. Most parents can be honest with themselves about their children's intelligence levels. So, be honest with yourself and ask if it might be worth insuring someone who doesn't know how to hand a plastic card to their medical providers. I'm sorry, I can't fix stupid.

These kids come into the pharmacy without insurance cards and pay hundreds of dollars out of pocket every month. When they're asked for insurance, they say they don't know about it. When they're told to ask their parents, they say they can't wait for the medication. HUNDREDS. CASH. OUT OF POCKET. How crazy is that? When I was in college, I ate ramen noodles because the McDonald's Dollar Menu was luxurious. Yet, these kids can afford hundreds for medications.

I'd like to clarify that as a pharmacy we do our due diligence. We ask for insurance cards, and we try to find the information before billing to cash. Please understand that there is nothing further we can do when the patient refuses to cooperate and demands to have their medication at any cost. You ask and you shall receive. This exchange also means a lot of angry parents will call me asking what the charges on their credit cards are for three-hundred dollars at the pharmacy. I can't magically pull insurance information down from a cloud and force your child to provide it to me. I always offer options, but the most convenient option is for the kid to pay cash. If you know the younger generation, then you know convenience is key.

Please educate your kids. Parents who sign up their college-bound kids at pharmacies and medical offices are the most responsible. I used to think it was crazy to have a twenty-year-old student's mom come into the pharmacy and give me the legal adult's information even though we cannot legally release medical information to the parent.

Kudos to the parents who know how unintelligent and incapable their children are. You are the people who make the most out of your insurance and save money.

And to the sophomore in college who gave me a scandalous pick up line and showed up later with his mom to register him as a patient, nice touch!

# Timing Is Everything

The essence of timing can change an entire transaction. When is the worst possible time to call someone? Reflect on the absolute worst time someone could call you during your day. Right when you wake up? When you lay in bed? Or when you are carrying five bags of groceries to your third-story walk-up or when you have to turn off a blaring alarm system? RING, RING. It's someone who needs to annoy you. If you agree that the worst time to call someone is when they're entering through a doorway, then why, OH WHY, do people insist on calling at 9:01 a.m. when stores open at 9:00 a.m.? Imagine we have just opened the gate, the registers are still booting up, there are prescriptions waiting to be filled, and then there's the phone call. I do not come to your office one minute after you get to work and demand assistance, so please do not come to mine.

To the people who wait behind the gate until I arrive at the store, I hope you stub your baby toe on the corner of a metal cabinet. Why would, better yet, how would the prescription that your doctor sent this morning be ready when you just watched me walk through the door? I understand there are people who need medications, but you saw me walk in. I'm not the Flash, and I'm not going to do some voodoo magic behind the pharmacy counter to have your medications ready in the next minute.

If I arrive at the store early and you're behind the gate, you will wait until we open. You do not get any special treatment just because you are here twenty minutes early. You basically just wasted twenty minutes of your own time. Eight out of ten days the registers are brought to me four minutes before the pharmacy opens. This timing means that even if I wanted to ring you up early, I couldn't.

**Patient:** *creeps into drive-through thirty minutes before opening on the one day the pharmacist arrives early. He has successfully pressed the assistance button four times*

**Pharmacist:** *lifts the "Closed" sign*

"We are closed for another thirty minutes."

**Excessively Annoying Patient:** "Can I get my medication now?"

**Irritated Pharmacist:** "No, we open in thirty minutes, and I can help you then."

**Excessively Annoying Patient:** "Why can't

you do it now? You're standing there."

**Irritated pharmacist:** *[what I wanted to say: "Shut your whore mouth or I will karate chop you."]*

"I don't have any registers back here at the moment, they will be on at 9:00 a.m."

**Excessively Annoying Patient:** "It is ridiculous you want me to wait thirty minutes for you to get your shit together."

<u>*PAUSE:*</u> *I know what you're thinking: He didn't actually cuss. Yes, he did. Because THAT is how people act around here. Also, is that ridiculous? Do you go to Pizza Hut demanding a pizza before they open? Do you go to the bank asking for money before the tellers arrive? If I come to your place of work (assuming he even works with that attitude), and I ask for something before you open, would I get served? None of your staff is there, your registers aren't up, it is just you walking through the door and getting bombarded with orders. Why is it more reasonable to wait outside of a clothing store in the mall to open than to wait at a pharmacy? It's not ridiculous, then, is it? People wait INSIDE of a Walmart on Black Friday for their displays to open, but that's not ridiculous, right? You are right sir; it is RIDICULOUS to wait for the pharmacy to even OPEN.*

**Excessively Annoying Patient:** *drives off in a rage only to return in thirty-two minutes*

**Irritated Pharmacist:** *rings him up as he is apologizing*

**Excessively Annoying Patient:** "I'm so sorry for my behavior. I wouldn't want anyone to talk to my girl that way, and if you were my girl, no one would ever talk to you like that."

**Irritated Pharmacist:** *[How? How did this just turn into a pick-up line?]*

*Side note: Why do people think it is okay to hit on people in retail settings? This is a pharmacy not a speed dating convention. Not to mention, I know all of your health issues (including the apparent mental ones). I hope you all understand hitting on your doctors is not the best idea because they know everything that is wrong with you, and trust me—it is not in any way, shape, or form to your benefit. I promise.*

· · ·

I walked in one Tuesday morning and the front store staff informed me there was an elderly man waiting for the pharmacy to open since 8:00 a.m. He kept saying it was an emergency as if he could convince the front staff to open the pharmacy for him. Upon opening the gates at 9:00 a.m., the man finally approached with his pharmacy request.

**Pharmacist:** *"Hi there, how can we help you?"* *[curious to see what the emergency was]*

**Impatient Patient:** "I need a refill, and I'll wait for it. How long will it take?"

**Pharmacist:** *grabs the bottle from his hand only to see it was for one Viagra *(commonly used for erectile dysfunction)* tablet*

"Give us fifteen to twenty minutes since our computers are still turning on now."

**Impatient Patient:** "Well, can you make it as soon as possible? I really need it, and I have to go!"

**Pharmacist:** "Well, of course we will try our best."

Instant thoughts: My Tuesdays are definitely not this exciting. If your Tuesday at 8:00 a.m. requires Viagra, then what does the rest of your week look like? And also, is there someone waiting for you at home? Massage parlor? Is there an appointment you're trying to meet? Hotel service? So many questions. Just one tablet does the trick for you? It's a low dose, and he is eighty-two years old. Perhaps he has a lady friend still asleep at home, and he used a tablet last night and would like another for the morning when she wakes up? Are you surprising someone with this tablet? I mean so, so, so many questions remain. One thing is for sure—your Tuesday was much better than mine, sir.

# Drive-Through Nightmares

There is a simple etiquette that should be maintained in public. Do you walk into your doctor's office smoking a cigarette and blowing smoke in their face? NO? Then why do you pull into my office (the drive-through) smoking in my face? A typical drive-through transaction lasts two to seven minutes. How is it possible one cannot wait five minutes to cruise out of the drive-through and light a cigarette? If you are in that desperate need of a smoke, then perhaps you should consider treatment.

Also, you should NOT be on speaker phone in the pharmacy drive-through. I PROMISE every worker and customer can hear what you are saying. I PROMISE. Even when you don't think the speaker is on, I will make sure it is. Do not pull into my office talking on the phone, holding your finger up, and telling me to wait a minute. You will suddenly see how busy I have gotten and that your wait time has increased ten to fifteen minutes.

COMMON COURTESIES PEOPLE.
Please learn and engage in these common courtesies.

Which brings me to my next mind-boggling thought: Why, OH WHY would one enter a drive-through lane when they see five other cars already in it? Consider that if each car requires about a five-minute transaction, you're going to reach at least the twenty five-minute mark. And yet you're upset that this should be a speedy service? Is five minutes not quick enough? Food for thought. When you see people ahead of you, go ahead and consider each car as a five-minute marker and come to terms with how long you may possibly wait. If you're not content with that wait time, I suggest you do something unheard of these days. . . . Park your car, use your left hand to lift the latch and open the door, slowly step out left foot then right foot, and travel to the pharmacy counter inside the store. It may not be well-known, but the inside of the store also offers functioning interfaces.

Did I mention the people who call from the drive-through? Ah yes, there's a group of special people who enter the line, decide they don't like the decision they just made, and want to talk to someone in the store about it. Without leaving the line. Now, these calls can go one of two ways. Either they want to see why their wait is "so long," or (the worst of the two) they want to add random items to their order.

**Lucky Caller Seventy-Nine**: *calls the pharmacy from the drive-through lane* "Hi, I want to pick up my medicine."

**Pharmacist**: "Okay, well it's ready for you

here, Lucky Caller Seventy-Nine."

**Lucky Caller Seventy-Nine**: "Okay, can you add some bacon with it too? I can't come inside right now, and I finished mine this morning."

**Pharmacist**: "Bacon . . .? This is the pharmacy; I don't have bacon."

**Lucky Caller Seventy-Nine**: "The store has bacon. Can't you just staple a pack to my bag and put it in the bin? The line is long—I'll come back for it tomorrow."

**Pharmacist**: "You can pick up your *medication* tomorrow, it'll be here for you. . . ."

Of all the things in all the worlds . . . bacon? And you want me to "staple it" to the prescription bag? And put it back in the bins? And then what . . . it just sits at room temperature until you've decided you need your bacon bad enough to come get it? Alright. Perfect idea.

# Part Two:
# Humanity's Downslope

# Sh*t People Say

## *Russian Roulette*

### Clearly Confused

**Exhausted Technician:** "Sir, since you didn't have any insurance, we put your prescription on a discount card. All you have to do is sign here to confirm that it was okay to register a discount card in your name."

**Confused Patient:** "Sign? I don't want to sign anything."

**Exhausted Technician:** "Sir, we can't use the discount card if you don't sign."

**Confused Patient:** "No, I don't sign. I don't have time for this. Take the discount off."

**Exhausted Technician:** "Okay, I can remove the discount; we will just need about fifteen minutes to rerun the prescriptions through the pharmacist."

**Confused Patient:** "Okay, I will wait."

This patient waited twenty-eight minutes total to *remove* a discount from his prescriptions, so he did not have to sign a piece of paper because he "didn't have time for it." So, you not only have to pay more, but you wait longer all under the premise of saving time? Alrighty. . . .

## Sketchy

A patient walks up to the counter with six liquid antipsychotic medication prescriptions while on the phone with her sister. Now, liquids are usually only special ordered as needed.

**Patient:** "I would like these filled."

**Pharmacist:** "Unfortunately, we don't have any of these in stock; they are special order items."

**Patient:** "You don't have any?"

**Pharmacist:** "No ma'am, but I can call around town and find it for you somewhere else if you would like."

**Patient:** "Okay."

**Pharmacist:** "The store *[2.4 miles]* down the street has them in stock and can fill it for you."

**Patient:** "No, I'm not driving to that side of town."

*proceeds to walk away talking to her sister*

"They didn't have any of them—it was sketchy."

Sketchy? Well, that was a first. I've never been called sketchy before. So, the new definition of sketchy is a pharmacy that does not carry special order medications on demand? Interesting. Also, 2.4 miles is not "the other side of town." This town is not five miles wide. The other store is closer than Target, Walmart, and Pizza Hut. So, I'm sure you're going to be going to one of those stores but not to get your medications.

## Can't Cure Stupid

5:10 p.m.: Patient calls in a medication

**Patient:** "I would like to pick up ___ medication in an hour."

**Pharmacist:** "Okay, we will have that ready for you."

*The medication is completed and put on the shelf, ready for pick up.*

5:25 p.m.: Patient calls back

**Patient:** "I got an automated call saying I have a prescription ready, and I would like to know what medication it is."

**Pharmacist:** *long dramatic silence followed by a sigh*

"It's the medication you just called in."

**Patient:** "Okay, but what's the name of it?"

REALLY? *Really.*

Surprisingly enough, this scenario happens often. I don't understand how so many people in one town can have amnesia. It blows my mind. Why do we have to reiterate and discuss the same information over and over again? Why are you wasting everyone's time? Are you bored? Lonely? Aren't there websites that can help with that?

## Ignorance Is the Light of Entertainment

**Patient:** *calls in regard to a recent company buyout*

"Why did you sell out?"

Honestly, I didn't even know what to say. Yeah, sorry, they offered ME $6 billion so I, MYSELF, made the decision alone. See, I work at this location just to keep my money hidden. I'm actually the billionaire decision maker for the company, and you caught me.

## No Talk Is Better than Small Talk

**Patient:** "It's beautiful outside, what are you doing in here?"

**Me:** "People keep coming so they told me I had to stay inside."

*we both awkwardly laugh, except deep down I hope

he gets a paper cut and squeezes a lemon on his way home*

## How Do You Live?

> **Patient:** "I just need to fill the one medication that needs to be filled."

> **Pharmacist:** "Which medication are you looking for? You have tons."

> **Patient:** "Well, I don't know the name, baby; I just need it filled."

I wish I could stress how many times a day people call for something, but they don't know the name or its use. Why are you even complaining if you don't know what you are treating? How do you even know you need it anymore?

## You People Annoy Me

> **Patient:** *on phone*

> "What can be filled?"

> **Pharmacist:** [*patient's profile list is longer than a*

*CVS receipt]* "Lots of things—what did you need?"

**Patient:** "Fill whatever can be filled, and I will pick what I want when I get there."

**Pharmacist:** "We only fill medications you need. I can't just fill and put back everything you don't want." *[technically I could, but that's a waste]*

**Patient:** "Fine. I'll get them, just fill it all."

*patient comes in a little while later demanding to know what is filled*

"Let me see which ones you filled."

*looks through eight medications*

"I'm not taking these two anymore. Why would you fill them?"

**Pharmacist:** " . . . Because you told me to fill anything that could be filled."

**Patient:** "But you should know I stopped taking these."

**Pharmacist**: "You didn't cancel the

prescriptions, so they were filled. I can put them back if you like."

**Patient:** "Put it all back; I just needed this ONE."

One. Out of eight medications, she chose one. If you call a pharmacy to get medications filled, then you should know which medications you want filled. Do not call hoping the staff will know all of your medications and which ones you are and are no longer taking. You are NOT our only patient. On an average day, our slowest pharmacy fills roughly 120 prescriptions. That is the equivalent to 840 prescriptions a week. If you assume that every patient has four prescriptions, that is 210 patients a week. Which means . . . you are not our only patient.

## Patient Calls

**Technician**: *calls a fifty-four-year-old woman to notify her that a prescription is ready for pickup*

**Patient:** "New phone, who dis?"

Really? That is how you answer a telephone? You are fifty-four years old. Please, act your age.

## Drive-Through

*A patient pulls into the drive-through, and the bell does not go off. Pharmacist does not see them until she turns around a few minutes later when she hears, "HONK!"*

> **Pharmacist:** "We have a bell to ring when you pull into the drive-through."

> **Patient:** "I know, I see it, I been here a thousand times."

> **Pharmacist:** *turns around to go get the prescriptions and then hears, "HONKKKKKKK!"*

FACEPALM. Why do people test my patience? I have no patience to begin with, and yet you insist on testing me? You, madame, are a sixty-three-year-old woman acting like a child. Impressive how petty some people can be when they're told they are wrong.

## TOO MUCH INFO

**Patient:** *walks out of the bathroom*

"PHEW! Almost didn't make it!"

Thank you, sir. That information was very vital to my existence.

## Cash Back?

*a patient is being checked out at the register*

**Pharmacist:** "Swipe your card for debit."

*swipes*

"Would you like cash back?"

**Patient:** *very serious face of concern*

"Where's it coming from?"

**Pharmacist:** "Your bank account . . . ."

**Patient:** "Oh, then no."

Did you think that the pharmacy was just giving

away free money and it was an option to choose whether or not you wanted some? Or that you won the lottery and I was the one letting you know? I mean, where, OH WHERE, did you think the money was coming from?

## Stupid Bitch

*A patient is being rung up at the register as she fumbles through her purse for her credit card. She opens a compartment of her purse and speaks to herself*

    **Patient**: "It's not in there, you stupid bitch."

*a hush fell over the pharmacy as we all tried to hold back our laughter*

    You called yourself a stupid bitch? OUT LOUD. For everyone to hear.

## GNM Part Two

*The same patient calls telling me she changed to a mail-order pharmacy and read in her new medication guide that the medication could affect her eyes. She wants to know if her eyeballs are going to fall out of the sockets*

## No Refund? No Problem

*A patient enters the drive-through, picks up Metformin, and leaves. Patient returns moments later saying the medication is the wrong brand and she MUST HAVE HER BRAND. This brand simply DOES NOT work*

Now, there is a semi-popular belief that medications of a different brand do not work the same. This is a MYTH, you crazy people. All medications that reach the shelves of the pharmacy are FDA approved, which means their potency was verified by someone with more than a high school education. So, ma'am who believes she knows all things, YES, it does work just the same.

Disclaimer: There are some medications that are *not* interchangeable. However, Metformin is not on that list.

*The patient returns to the drive-through window to insist that she can only use a single brand, one we no longer carry. It is a product our wholesaler does not provide. Upon our sharing this information with her, the world collapsed. Time stopped*

> **Patient:** "Well, what do you expect me to do?"

> **Me:** "The medication provided to you is bio

equivalent to the medication you were taking before. Therefore, it will work just as well."

**Patient:** "No, it doesn't work. This is ridiculous! You want me to DIE?"

*pauses for dramatic effect*

**Me:** *smirks and laughs*

"If you find another pharmacy who is able to order your brand for you, I can transfer your medication. In the meantime, I can give you the few tablets of this specific brand I have left."

**Patient:** "NO. I don't want ANYTHING from you. I'm gonna call my doctor, and if something happens to me, YOU will be liable."

Now, I should mention Metformin is used to treat diabetes. This specific patient has manageable diabetes; however, she chooses not to change her lifestyle and instead badgers her doctors. Not only can she not take responsibility for her medication and disease state, she also needs someone to blame. I should mention I am not liable in any form for whatever may happen to said patient. The medication was PROVIDED and REFUSED. That, my friend, is a personal choice.

How do you prevent this kind of situation if you're

one of those batshit crazy people who needs one specific brand of a very common medication?

## How to Get What You Want from a Pharmacy

1. Let your pharmacy know you are not open to changing between manufacturers.

2. Contact the pharmacy EARLY before your next refill. Don't wait until you've been without the medication for three days.

3. TAKE RESPONSIBILITY FOR YOUR OWN HEALTH CARE. You *cannot* expect others to care as much about your health care as you do. That is not feasible. At the end of the day; the pharmacists leave work, go home, and don't bat an eyelash about you or your problems. So, if you need something, find it and make it happen.

4. STOP BLAMING OTHERS. If you're batshit crazy; then accept it, admit it, and move on. Don't blame other people for your possible, alleged, far-fetched DEATH, crazy. Your lack of lifestyle change has worsened this situation, and yet . . . I am liable for your lack of exercise and the fast food in the front seat? Did I force feed you all that ice cream like the freezer was broken?

# Utterly Uncomfortable

Some days, being the boss really pays off when all I do is seek entertainment. I initiated a onesie-Wednesday on a week where all the kids (my lovely technicians) dressed up in their favorite onesies to celebrate . . . comfort?

*A patient enters the drive-through to pick up a prescription. Female pharmacy technician, in a rather comfortable cow onesie, approaches to aid the customer. There is a little small talk and exchanges are made*

**Patient**: "I wish I could milk your udders."

Now . . . let's discuss. Why? Why is this statement considered appropriate? Why do men—gross older men at that—think it is okay to hit on working young women? She's a pharmacy technician locked and loaded with all of your medical history knowledge. Let's just say, the odds are never in your favor when you're hitting on medical professionals who tend to your health needs.

## Jailbird

*patient calls the pharmacy all day, back and forth*

**Patient:** "What can be filled?"

**Pharmacist:** "I don't have anything on your profile, which means we haven't filled for you for over 1.5 years—everything would be expired."

**Patient:** "No its not, it's cuz I was locked up, but I'm back. You can fill it again."

**Pharmacist:** "We can't fill expired medications; you need a new prescription."

**Patient:** "Okay, but I don't wanna get locked up again."

...

That summer, we had a patient's spouse call stating her husband had just been released from prison and needed their medications. She said he was in poor health and that no one contacted him since his recent release about his medications. After having this discussion multiple times, we told her to contact the prison doctor or establish a new provider to send in new prescriptions. Turns out the gentleman was released in January of that year, and he was only covered under the prison for the month of release. He waited six months to begin reaching out for medical assistance and thought that we advised him to go back to jail to get medications.

## Old Man Chronicles

Flu season can be hectic for many of us who usher hundreds of people through the vaccine gates a day. I particularly enjoyed it when it was the flu (only-flu) season where we could vaccinate and get to know s-o-m-e people. I had an elderly gentleman in his early eighties who I called to the pharmacy for a vaccine, but he did not respond. A few minutes later, he walked up to the counter and said he was ready now.

> **Old Man:** "I apologize; I was in the restroom."

> **Pharmacist:** "No problem at all."

*begins vaccinating*

> "Are you having a good day?"

> **Old Man:** "Yes, it was fine. But forgive me, I am quite old and frail these days."

> **Pharmacist:** "Oh, that's nonsense."

*nervous laughter. Completes the vaccine*

> **Old Man:** *stands up to leave*
>
> "No really, forgive me, I really needed to use the bathroom, but I didn't realize it in time and it just kind of snuck up on me."
>
> **Pharmacist:** "No worries, we got your vaccine done in time."

Now at this point, I didn't think twice about it. I assumed he was apologizing for the delay, which was very kind of him.

*five minutes later*

> **Customer:** "Someone took a huge shit on the floor of the men's room and walked through it into the hallway."

Well, he did apologize.

## Had Too Much

We once had a practicing pharmacist who was in her eighties. Now, you may think this is unsafe (and you're probably right), but she was the best. The best person to stand up for you. The best person to tell a customer how it is. And the best person to set someone straight.

*A young gentleman enters the pharmacy area swaying back and forth, barely standing up in line. As he gets closer to the front, he is standing half hunched over, half drooling. Unable to keep his balance when he gets to the front counter, he holds himself up with the register*

> **Young Man:** "Can I get a pack of one-CC-twenty-nine-gauge needles?"

> **Technician:** *visibly uncomfortable; grabs the pharmacist*

> "One moment please."

> **Pharmacist:** "What was it you needed, honey?"

> **Young Man:** *standing half up*

> "One-CC-twenty-nine-gauge needles."

**Pharmacist:** "Honey, I think you've already had enough of whatever you're using."

Much to everyone's shock, the man left without another word.

Disclaimer: Needle laws vary state to state, but the right to sell needles varies with pharmacist discretion. While there are pros and cons to both sides, this is not CNN debate center.

# You Are Not My Only Patient

There are annoying people in any retail setting. Some are worse than others, but I firmly believe that some of these people only behave this way when they enter a pharmacy—or better yet, drive up to a pharmacy (we all know how difficult it can be to stand up and walk inside to discuss your health care at the ripe age of twenty).

To the people who drive up to the pharmacy asking for a prescription written by "Dr. Smith," you are not our only patient, and you are not the only patient for "Dr. Smith," AND there is not only one "Dr. Smith." SO PLEASE CLARIFY LIKE AN INTELLIGENT PERSON.

**Unidentified Patient:** "I'm here to pick up."

*silent stare*

**Annoyed Pharmacist:** *[okay, cool. . . .]* "Okay, who are you picking up for?"

**Unidentified Patient:** "Becky."

**Annoyed Pharmacist:** *[seriously? A first name is all you give? Because you're the only Becky in this whole state?]*

"Becky who?"

**Unidentified Patient:** *irritated with the question*

A proper healthcare introduction includes the patient's full name, date of birth, and what you would like to achieve. This is not rocket science. You do not walk into a doctor's office giving them attitude when they ask for your date of birth. You don't get mad when Pizza Hut asks for your name. So why, OH WHY, is it so hard to do the same at the pharmacy? THIS is why people end up spending more time in the pharmacy. When you have a conversation like every piece of information is dragged out of you like you're under hefty government interrogation, it is extremely difficult to get anything done.

While we are on the subject, let's discuss my other pet peeve: when we are helping a customer and you yell from twenty feet away over the person we are helping. Hi, hello, how do you expect to be helped if we are already helping someone else? You just thought it was a good idea to yell? Maybe you'll get a response faster? I love that the people who do yell, they always do it because, "It'll be real quick." Well, who's to say your needs are more important? Or you'll be done quicker than the person ahead of you?

...

A Lady (we'll call her Scentsy Sue) spends twenty minutes ringing her stuff up, chatting about her life, smelling the entire waiting area. Not causing a smell, mind you, she lifts miscellaneous items and sniffs them. Pamphlets, medicine bottles, hand sanitizer, whatever in her reach. After her transaction ends, she proceeds to talk through her sniffing journey. The cashier slowly tries to pull away from the situation and eventually succeeds. Moments later, we are helping another patient, and she returns with a vengeance.

*A customer is standing at the register. Pharmacist is consulting*

**Scentsy Sue:** *twenty feet away*

"HEY! HEYYY!!! HEYYYY!!!!!!!!!!!!!!"

**Pharmacist:** "We will be with you in a moment."

**Scentsy Sue:** *volume ten*

"HEY I JUST WANT TO TELL YOU—"

**Pharmacist:** "Ma'am, we are currently helping someone; we will be with you in a moment."

**Scentsy Sue:** "WELL, I WANT TO TELL YOU THAT YOU GON' HAVE TO CALL SOMEONE! I BLEW THEM BATHROOMS UP AND IT WON'T FLUSH!"

Thank you so much, Scentsy Sue. Thank you for not only telling me but the entire store that you shat in our bathroom. For announcing not only how rude but nasty you are, thank you Sue.

# Coupon Nancies

COUPONS are what hold up lines. COUPONS are what keep you waiting. NOT the people trying to use them for your benefit. Next time you are in line with ten prescription coupons for the one item and are wondering what is taking so long, know that YOU are the reason the transaction is taking ten times longer than it should.

For those of you who do not have insurance and are looking for good deals, prescription coupons are great, but they are not set-in-stone prices. These prices can vary with every refill. Take a moment and digest that: every refill can be a different price . . . because they said so. Some of you are probably shaking your head or wondering, "Why?"

Because they can. Those coupons are a privilege, NOT A RIGHT. They are doing you a favor by offering you a discount. You are not their gift; they are your gift. No pharmacy is required to use coupons. In fact, many pharmacies do not prefer to use coupons. Some flat out deny the use of coupons. These cards are in no way a benefit to the pharmacy. A lot of times, the pharmacy is losing money, in the form of time and productivity, by using them.

*Side note: It is completely unreasonable to expect a pharmacy personnel to run multiple (sometimes upwards of ten) different discount cards to find you the cheapest price. Sorry, but that is not my job, and as you may have learned from my earlier chapter, you are not my only patient. Out of the kindness of our hearts, we will run various cards to find a better deal, if time permits. However, there are patients who DEMAND multiple cards be tested. No ma'am, that is not how that works. If you find a unicorn (tolerant, kind pharmacist willing to run ten different discount cards on eight different medications), then at least have the courtesy to give them time to run the prescriptions. Do not arrive during rush hour expecting them to run eighty different transactions.*

Lady walks up to the pharmacy counter for a prescription refill*

> **Needy Lady:** "I need five refills. I'd like to wait, and I normally use a discount card."

> **Pharmacist:** "Okay, well the price has gone up on the discount card from last time."

> **Needy Lady:** "They usually run a bunch of different ones to find the cheapest price this time. I refer all my friends to your store because you guys always run all my cards."

Now, any small retailer would love the referrals and business, but as a large chain, no. We do not love the waste of time.

> **Annoyed Pharmacist:** "I can run multiple cards for you, but it will take time."

> **Needy Lady:** "Well, I have about ten or fifteen minutes, so I'll wait here."

You guys should know when you run five scripts with five different discount cards, you have twenty-five transactions about to occur. Twenty-five transactions take more than ten minutes.

> **Annoyed Pharmacist:** "I will run the cards, but I should warn you, they do not replace insurance and will not be accepted at all times."

> **Needy Lady:** "I will transfer pharmacies if they're not accepted anymore, and I have been here for ten-plus years."

> **Annoyed Pharmacist:** [*please transfer. Just go. Music to my ears. Don't tease me*]

"We would be sad to see you go."

*holding back a large grin*

*Side note: If you threaten to transfer pharmacies, doctors, or facilities because you don't like their policies, chances are the employees will be overjoyed to see you leave. They will probably throw a party at the idea of you threatening to leave. If you threaten them and their face lights up, please don't tease them. Just go already. Hardly ever are people upset to see you go. Sometimes we push people to leave. If I were a statistician or cared enough, I'd show you statistics on how when you don't waste one hour running discount cards for one patient, we can fill and tend to more prescriptions. It is in our benefit to lose some time consuming business. You're lucky I'm too lazy for numbers; I'm more of a rant-er.*

...

Discount cards are a gift. They are not a right; they are a privilege. You do not walk into a restaurant and tell them to scan any coupon they can find (not even bothering to bring your own coupon), so do not walk into my pharmacy like Queen Sheba and think that this schtick will work. We do not control the fluctuation of prices. When someone gives you a gift, you don't yell at them. You graciously thank them for their effort (whether or not it was beneficial).

Due to a high number of unsatisfied, ungracious, and (frankly) rude customers, most pharmacy employees do not bother with coupon cards anymore. When we say we've run them all and given you the best deal, what we mean is we put it on a discount card and don't have time for your attitude.

To my front store coupon folks, if you are a hardcore coupon junkie, that is amazing . . . for you. However, I couldn't care less about your hunt or what deals are out there. I am also not a cashier or certified bag person. With that being said, our open register does not mean it is for regular customers and even worse— Coupon Nancies. I will NOT go above and beyond to make your coupons work. I am a pharmacist, not a registered magician. I do not care what the shelf says. I do not care what the newspaper advertises and I do not care if the application on your phone told you it was in the store. If you walk up to my register, be prepared to pay whatever price it rings up, or go to the front store registers, where the cashiers are specifically trained to help you. Do not waste the pharmacy's time with your coupon disasters.

# Types of People

We all know there are many different types of people. As we grow up, we find there are differences created by socioeconomic classes, cultures, neighborhoods, and zodiac signs. But did you know there are different kinds of stupid? Science (that's my nickname for now) has proven that there are, in fact, different types of stupid.

## Types of People Who Annoy Me:

1.  The person who has to leave with something: I loathe these people! When you come in and ask for one specific thing, you can't have it, then ask for something completely unrelated, don't have that, and ask for something else. We have patients who start out looking for pain medications but leave with nasal spray because they HAVE TO HAVE SOMETHING. JUST LEAVE. STOP WASTING OUR TIME BECAUSE YOU'RE UNSATISFIED.

2. The whisperer: In the age where masks are predominantly worn everywhere, why whisper? You whisper behind a mask, a face shield, a register guard, and with a loud crowd of people behind you. SPEAK UP. We don't have time for this! In addition, if you are in the passenger seat while at a drive-through for pickup, then have the driver answer for you—WE CAN'T HEAR YOUR WHISPERS FROM THERE. Nine out of ten drivers act like they have no idea what is going on when they enter the drive-through. The look on their face is as if they've been drugged and woke up in the drive-through without any recollection of how they got there.

3. The drive-through stop sign: After many years of trial and error with the drive-through, we finally came to the conclusion that there is no solution to help make a drive-through more pleasant. My pet peeve is when I walk into the pharmacy in the morning with coffee in hand, hair in a top bun to avoid brushing, and a small glimmer of hope that today won't be as bad as yesterday, until . . . yup. Someone is parked in the drive-through. Ten minutes before opening, parked doing their morning ritual in our drive-through. Its 7:50 a.m. . . . What could possibly be so important at 7:50 a.m.? Why didn't you finish your morning routine at home instead of dry shaving in the drive-through?

Solutions? About two years ago, we put up a sign at closing each night stating: "Pharmacist is not on duty, you may not park in the drive-through while the pharmacy is closed." I refer to this as a social experiment because it shows how creative people can be. To enforce this policy, we would greet people parked two minutes before opening and let them know they could pull around when the pharmacy opened, and this is what we found:

1.  You have the guy who didn't see the sign after sitting there for twenty-plus minutes.

2.  The woman who says, "Well, you open in four minutes anyways, so I can wait here." *Nope. In fact, I just told you that you can't wait there.*

3.  The person who really, really needs their ADHD medications because they have an exam and really needs to study, so can we just give it to them now because we are here already. . . . *No, I just told you we aren't in the mood to work yet, so come back when we have to work, thanks.*

4.  The man who was upset that we told him to pull around the building and back into the drive through when we opened, so he parked at the back of the drive-through to be the FIRST person in line at 8:00 a.m. . . . *He actually created a line of cars starting fifty feet from the drive-through line, and not a single car questioned waiting behind him. Ten minutes early. Geniuses*

*leading geniuses, I say.*

5.  Lastly, the child-like person who pretends not to hear you so you have to roll the window up, show your face, and motion for them to leave

# Part Three:
# The Never Ending Spiral

# Untold Stories

## You're Welcome for Keeping You Alive

*Ms. Thaaaaang walks up with two seizure prescriptions for a two-year-old child. The pharmacy does not have either medication in stock*

> **Pharmacist:** "Unfortunately, we do not have either medication in stock at this location, however, there is another location 1.8 miles away that is willing to stay open and fill this medication for you. Or, if you have enough at home for tonight and tomorrow, I could order it to come in two days from now."

> **Bad Mother:** "Just order it. I'm sick of driving around town."

> **Concerned Pharmacist:** "Do you have enough medication for tonight and the next day?"

**Bad mother:** "No, I am tired of driving around. Just order it like I said."

**Concerned Pharmacist:** *[child safety whistles blowing left and right]* "I advise you to take this to the other pharmacy. They will stay open and fill it for you since it concerns the welfare of a child."

**Bad mother:** "I'm tired of you people sending me all around town. I'm sick of driving around today. This is just ridiculous."

*storms off*

Really? Is it ridiculous to be concerned about a two-year-old child newly discharged from the hospital? I'm sorry I tried to keep your child from having a seizure, which in turn keeps you out of the emergency room since you're sick of driving. Even worse, I'm sorry I tried to keep your child alive.

Also, anyone who works in retail knows the last half hour of the night before a store closes is wrap up time. You work on end of day tasks, clean up, and sort out messes. So, you're welcome, Bad Mother, for trying to help you while I could have easily ordered the medication and not thought about it twice. You are welcome for trying to keep your child alive, you ass.

## Not So Common Sense

The younger population's lack of knowledge on how to handle themselves stems from generations of stupid.

A patient calls the pharmacy YELLING about a Hydrocodone prescription. Apparently, she did not receive the correct amount upon pickup. The lady should have received ninety tablets but says there was NO WAY she could have taken forty tablets already. Luckily, the pharmacy has cameras set on counting stations that allow us to verify prescriptions have been filled properly. Being the studious worker I am, I call the patient back to let them know that the manager needs some time to check the cameras; however, we will notify them as soon as we verify everything on our end.

> **Delusional Patient:** "Okay, well there is no way I took forty tablets. I mean, I took 2.5 tablets Friday, 3 Saturday, and 2 Sunday. That's it. I haven't taken it anymore. See, my neighbor has stolen them from me before. I caught him in my shed, once. I even saw he stole my toilet brush before."

> **Pharmacist:** "Okay . . . well, we will call you as soon as we know something."

> **Delusional Patient:** "Alright, and I mean, there are about fifty or so left in this bottle,

and I put some in a pill pack thing—"

**Pharmacist:** "Ma'am, can you count how many tablets you have there?"

**Delusional Patient:** "Like right now? It's about fifty. I need to find the tablets because I hid them."

**Pharmacist:** ". . . Yeah, if you could count them, it would really help us with verifying the correct fill."

**Delusional Patient:** *counts tablets and comes back*

"It's eighty-one, so just a few more than fifty."

**Pharmacist:** *[if you took 6.5 tablets, how do you have a whole number of tablets left? And how is eighty-one a bit more than fifty?]*

"Well ma'am, if you have eighty-one there, and you took 6.5 tablets—"

**Delusional Patient:** "Well no, I don't have 81—I have a half tablet, its 79.5"

**Pharmacist:** *[how did 81 turn into 79.5 when she*

*subtracted half a tablet?]*

"Regardless, you would have—"

**Delusional Patient:** "See, I dropped the bottle on the floor, but I think I got them all up. I don't think I saw any go under the fridge."

**Pharmacist:** *[ . . . you're kidding me, right? You dropped them, think they're stolen, took some (but don't know how many), and are now accusing me of shorting them?]*

"Well ma'am, if you have eighty-one, and you took roughly seven tablets already—"

**Delusional Patient:** "Well I just took another one because this is stressing me out."

**Pharmacist:** "That means you had eighty-eight tablets at some point and possibly dropped two tablets—"

**Delusional Patient:** "It's not dropped, I know someone don' stole them. I'ma find out if they still live across the street because they don' stole it."

**Pharmacist:** "Okay, well we will call you when we confirm the count on our end."

**Delusional patient:** *continues to ramble
until finally tiring self out enough to hang up*

One of the worst things you can do is to call
someone and accuse them of making a mistake without
actually verifying if that's true. When any patient calls
and starts the conversation with, "I picked up my
prescription Friday, and there's a mistake," everyone's
heart drops. No matter where you work, your heart will
drop. What if we actually *did* make that mistake? Was
it deadly? Was anyone hurt? Are we losing our jobs?
So many thoughts trail through our minds that we can
barely catch our breath before the patient finishes their
story. However, if you want to scam a pharmacy into
giving you more items because you think you can, rest
assured, some of us are battling this notion to the core.
There are cameras watching the fill station to make
sure no one is stealing and that the correct amount and
medication is dispensed. Precautions have been put
in place, and I promise pharmacies will come up with
more and more roadblocks to ensure no one steals or
walks away with free medications

## Sorry I Helped

There are some instances in the pharmacy world where
I feel kind and giving. Usually, within five minutes, my
regret sets in.

*A man arrived with two prescriptions that were

greater than $700 on insurance. I found a discount for both medications, bringing the total down to fifteen dollars. I spend upwards of twenty-five minutes signing up the patient for the discount card programs to ensure he is able to get this good deal*

**Proud Pharmacist:** *beaming with pride*

"I was able to get a discount card for your medications, bringing the total from $700 down to just $15!"

*[pats self on the back]*

**Ungrateful Patient:** "Okay, but what about next time?"

*[unphased by a $685 saving]*

**Disappointed Pharmacist:** "Well, sir, it will be that price for one year."

**Ungrateful Patient:** "Oh okay, that's good I guess."

Really? No thank you? No surprise? No praise? No grateful attitude at all? Well, next time, that prescription just may be $700 due to some miraculous deletion of the discount cards. You put no effort into your own money savings, and you aren't even thankful to someone who took the time to do that for you? Impressive how numb our society has become to help.


## You're Disgusting


The number of people who miss the toilet amazes me. I mean, the bowl isn't very small. Toilets don't vary in size much. Between cultures, worldwide, people sit and pee in a hole. Simple. Apparently, it's not simple enough.

*A woman goes to the store's public restroom and comes out in a hurry*

> **Hysterical Woman:** "Someone rubbed shit all over the wall."

> **Pharmacist:** *[confused as to why someone would exaggerate to that extent]*

"We will have someone look into that. . . ."

Sure enough, there was human feces in the shape of a handprint against the wall of the toilet stall. It was rubbed against the wall like someone was trying to paint with their own stool. How do these things happen? Dissect the situation for a moment: someone took a shit, consciously put their hand in it, then rubbed their hand against the wall to paint a mural. Did they wash their hands when they were done? How did they pull their pants up with shitty hands? Where was the toilet paper? Was this because they were waiting too long in the pharmacy? What would possess someone to put their hand in a toilet and touch their own shit? People are disgusting.

A sales associate tells me all the bathrooms are closed until further notice. Now, this is a common occurrence. Typically, bathrooms are closed if they need to be cleaned for the day or if the supplies need replenishing. After further investigation, I find out that someone has successfully *shat* on the bathroom floor. Yes, you read that correctly. Someone entered a three-stall public restroom, stood in front of the sink, faced the mirror, and decided here was where she was going to defecate. She then proceeded to stand up, and we can only assume she didn't wash her hands since she took a shit in front of the sink.

Immediately I think, how? How does someone mistake the floor for a toilet? Or not make it to the toilet that is four feet to the left? It seems like it may have been on purpose, so then, why? Why would someone hate our store so much? Waited too long? Bad customer service? Items out of stock? What could make you so angry that you'd take a shit on a public floor?

People disgust me.

...

One day a pharmacist and store manager retreated to the store's breakroom for a quick managers meeting. After a few seconds there was an unbearable smell that overtook the room. An extensive expedition for the stench lead to finding a shit someone had taken in the trash can, of the breakroom.

Now, how did anyone get back there? Was it an employee? An employee wouldn't do that because they use this room too, right? Or, did someone quit today and we haven't noticed yet? Did a customer just meander to the break room for this purpose?

Too many questions and more disgust.

## This Is Not My Job

Have you ever had a request so outlandish from someone and thought, "That is not my job!"? In retail, this thought occurs every hour. Every hour for twelve hours in a row, people suggest, request, or demand things that are far from our jobs. Again, these are real requests from people who consider themselves intelligent.

*lady calls the pharmacy demanding to speak to the pharmacist for an emergency situation*

**Lady:** "We picked up an antibiotic for my son the other day. I was wondering if diarrhea is a side effect?"

**Pharmacist:** "Yes ma'am, diarrhea is a possible side effect of this medication. It is important to—"

**Concerned Mother:** "Yeah, yeah, I've got his shit under control, but I'm ticked off because he got in trouble at school."

**Pharmacist:** "Okay. . . ."

**Concerned Mother:** "He had to use the bathroom, and the school wouldn't let him use it, then they sent him to the counselor's office and he had a real smart aleck attitude, and I'm ticked off."

**Pharmacist:** "Alright—"

**Concerned Mother:** "I'm filing a lawsuit, and I need you to write a letter stating that diarrhea is a possibility, and it's why he had to use the bathroom."

**Pharmacist:** " . . . "

**Concerned Mother:** "And I need it now because they're not going to stop my baby from letting it out."

**Pharmacist:** " . . . Well, ma'am, you can Google the side effects of that medication for proof or ask your doctor for a letter. However, at the retail level, we cannot provide that kind of documentation."

**Concerned Mother:** "Okay, thank you, I'm just real ticked off because of this shit."

A lot of times while working in retail, you find that people cannot separate departments of stores, even if they are separate entities. Imagine walking into one of those Walmarts that has a bank and asking the bank teller if they had a specific brand of toilet paper in stock. Why would he even know that? That bank is independent of Walmart—it just so happens to be there. Similarly, we get asked many crazy questions to which people cannot fathom why we have no answers. So, I'd like to go on record and say:

NO, we do not know if there is more of your favorite candy in the back.

NO, we do not know why the photo order you put in fifteen minutes ago hasn't finished yet.

NO, we do not know why one size of the wine bottles is on sale but not the other.

NO, we do not know when the seasonal candles arrive.

NO, we do not know if the makeup you wear is on our next truck order.

NO, we do not know how to install the shower handle even though the store sells the item.NO, we cannot allow you to open and try the socks on before you buy them to make sure they feel good.

These are not part of the pharmacy's tasks. Some of these items aren't even part of the front store's tasks. There are some things you as a consumer have to do on your own. Stop being lazy, and search for the answer yourself. Every store has a telephone app that shows you their inventory, so you don't have to ask a clerk to find something for you when you can see it is out of stock. Use your resources and think through your questions before asking the store because there is such a thing as a stupid question. There may not have been in previous times, but in modern society, this population is full of dumbass questions.

# I Don't Care

Honestly, I JUST DON'T CARE. Please understand—your life problems, your vacations, your urges to use the bathroom—DO NOT matter to me.

*Side note: My life does not suddenly brighten because you are going to Costa Rica tomorrow. Go punch yourself if you tell your pharmacist you need your medications because you're going on some elaborate vacation while we have to work. It's like when the waiter brings food and says enjoy and I reply with, "You too." Ultimate facepalm. Why would they enjoy food while they're working?!*

For about a month, I had a patient who would call the pharmacy every day and ask if her blood pressure was good (which it always was) and then ask if her sugar was good (she never had a reading; she would just tell me what she ate). One week in particular, she called every single day. This carried on for ten days in a row.

**Pharmacist**: *answers telephone*

"Thanks for calling the pharmacy, how can I help you?"

**Patient**: "HEY."

**Pharmacist**: "Hey, how can I help you?"

**Patient**: "I POOPED TODAY."

**Pharmacist**: "Oh wow, that's . . . great."

**Patient**: "Yeah . . . I tried really hard."

**Pharmacist**: "Do you need medication so you don't have to try so hard?"

**Patient**: "No, I scoop it out when I need to."

**Pharmacist**: *speechless*

It is a common misconception that people in the service industry want to hear about your life. Our companies pride themselves on fast and friendly service. When you get the smile, multiple nods, and a few mmhmmms; just end the conversation. We aren't listening, we don't care, and we don't need an explanation.

On multiple occasions, we have had various pharmacists question a particular patient's medication regimen. Now, there are many people who are sticklers for dispensing certain medications, but I'd like to think I'm pretty understanding. When the seventeen-year-old on three different doses of Methylphenidate came across my radar . . . well, I had a few questions.

> **Mother:** I know that you guys had questioned his dose before, but if you knew my son, you'd give him even more."

> **Pharmacist:** I understand. However, we have to make sure that the patient is taking appropriate doses for their own safety and well-being. Also, keeping up with all these medications cannot be easy. It may be better to look into a different medication regimen that is more effective and manageable."

> **Mother:** "Yeah, it's something I'll talk to the doctor about eventually. If you knew my son, you'd know he's kind of crazy. He's seventeen and 289 pounds and he can lift me up like it's nothing. I'm 190 pounds and he doesn't even bat an eyelash lifting me up. Him and his brother both, but his brother is older. That's kind of crazy that they're so young and can just pick me up. Well, not in a weird way, not abusing or sexual. And you know he is large, but that small afternoon dose really brings him back down enough to do his homework

and calm down enough before bed. I can't deal with him if I he doesn't take all three— it's a nightmare. Sometimes, I just have to walk away even when he is medicated. But I thank you guys for trying to help, maybe you can help by throwing a few extra in there too."

*insert Southern aggressive laughter*

...

Now, how do I stress to someone that we just don't need all of that information about their household? Also, sometimes when you volunteer information, it may take a second for us to look into your medications to identify whatever it is you're referring to. This action can lead to even more problems for you like further investigating or red flags we may have overlooked. It's always easier to cut your life stories short, ask for what you need, and move on. Find new friends. Perhaps join a friend-finder app online? Maybe join a book club? Reconnect with a long-lost friend?

But I cannot be your friend.

## Insulin and the Tales We Tell

Every state, company, and pharmacist have their own insulin syringe policy. Some people believe that if you are going to shoot up drugs, you should at least have a clean needle and prevent the risk of disease. Others believe that giving the needle enables drug usage and spreads the epidemic. Honestly, both sides are understandable, so we have long given these decisions to those selling the needles. If you are comfortable, sell it. If you are not comfortable, find someone who is, or tell them where they can find clean needles hassle free. Many of you may not agree with this tactic, but it is what has been agreed upon across a large staff, and it has worked for many years.

What don't we want to do? Listen to your stories.

*person approaches the pick-up counter*

> **Person**: "I need to get insulin needles for my grandma's Warfarin."

> **Cashier**: *obviously confused, trying to contain their response and steer the conversation*

> "What size?"

> **Person**: "Two milligrams, Warfarin."

For those of you who don't know, Warfarin is a TABLET. Also, why'd you ask for "insulin needles" and not just say it is for insulin instead of Warfarin? That leads me to believe you don't know what insulin is, you just think "insulin needle" is the name of the needle. Lastly, needles come in a variety of lengths and milliLITER dispensing sizes. At least try to learn some numbers that could apply?

*Facepalm*

# Thoughts of a Pharmacist

Some days are better than others. We all know this fact, but there are some days where all the stupid comes out to play at once. It doesn't have to be Friday the 13th to have bad luck around the pharmacy. A full moon doesn't have to shine upon us for crazies to emerge.

Have you ever noticed in movies there is never just one zombie roaming the streets for brains? They are always traveling in packs. Well, packs are also how people travel into pharmacies. In herds—like cattle but less organized. It's like people form flash mobs in the parking lot, and when they get a good ten folks together (plus another three who have insurances issues; maybe two who need transfers from a pharmacy in Puerto Rico; and one special person who needs their blue pill from a pharmacy back home because they are here on vacation, and their pharmacy is closed, and we don't know what the magic blue pill does), ONLY THEN do they all enter our doors.

Pro tip: If you see only one person working in the pharmacy, hear the phones ringing bloody murder, see others standing around like they are waiting for a circus show to begin; don't try to wait. Do not convince yourself you will be in and out of there in ten minutes. Do not let the Pizza Hut mentality fool you into adding a member to the audience. Leave and come back later. It is ALWAYS in everyone's best interest for you to come back later.

If you approach a pharmacy counter and don't see anyone, the pharmacists see you. Wait patiently. They'll come to you. No need for you to lean half your beer belly over the counter to see who is back there. You don't have to "YOOO HOOOO" or "HELLLLOOO" us. We see you; we hear you; we ignore you the more you do that. It will take an extra ten seconds to help you solely because I will not be rushed. Call me spiteful, but with so many tasks and only two hands, I'll get to you when I can, sir. Comments like, "I didn't know if anyone was back there," are a waste of your breath and a true display of your own stupidity. You thought that we just abandoned the pharmacy midday, gates open, drugs on display? We just . . . ran away? Quit? Zombie apocalypses hit and we were eaten but you survived to tell the tale? Funny joke, Jim; a ten-second wait should be expected for every dull comment.

# Note from a Pharmacist

One thing that other healthcare professionals may not understand is that retail pharmacy lacks the luxury of time. When there is no time there are no cushy resources that we were taught to use on clinical rotations or quick evidence based medicine research. Logging into those websites lasts longer than any patient's attention span. You need an answer NOW. So, that level of knowledge—that need for on-demand clinical skills from drug interactions, to diagnosing physical conditions when someone lifts their shirt in public and points to a rash isn't easy. It isn't easy, it isn't pretty, and it certainly isn't effortless. We are nothing if not the multitaskers of a lifetime!

As pharmacists, our greatest fault is that we have not banded together in support of each other. I often hear complaints about other pharmacists and their habits or how they run their stores. Considering every store has its own unique situation, we are not in a place to judge one another but much rather to uplift each other. It is our duty to support each other and share our adventures to bring light to the darkest days. Finding the humor in our everyday lives gives us the strength to move forward.

As I have shared my experiences, I hope that you understand the depth of the pharmacy profession. There are many different sectors of pharmacy and we each face our own challenges and rewards. Retail pharmacy is more patient facing and based on immediate external as well as internal stress. I encourage everyone to challenge themselves and sympathize with the white coats behind the counter. Listen to your pill slinging friends when they speak, sometimes, it's entertaining.

# COVID-19

It's funny how what was once a cartoon episode reference became a world-wide pandemic. It seems like overnight, our entire lives just changed for the worse. Even more people grew privileged fairy wings and now prance around town littering the public with their damned attitudes. The aggression among people who have been confined to their own company for months is unbelievable. YOU DON'T EVEN LIKE TO BE WITH YOU. Perhaps it's something to think about—if you don't enjoy time with yourself, why would anyone else enjoy you terrorizing them in public?

On that note:

To the Karens who earned the name through the haircut: Please stay home.

To the parent whose child is knocking every last item off the shelves as they scream bloody murder: Please stay home.

To the "dog parent" whose "dog child" is peeing in

aisle twelve: Please stay home.

To the man who came to pick up a medication for his child because his wife told him to; and he doesn't remember the child's date of birth, insurance, or phone number: Please stay home.

To the elderly gentleman who can't hear through "these stupid government requirements"

(Masks) and pulls it down to get in your face: Please stay home.

...

It is unbelievable how the country that stayed home for months still had not gotten their lives together when they were released again. It is as if they came back with a vengeance . . . of stupidity.

Looking back on March 2020 when the majority of the United States shut down and businesses slowly dwindled, do you remember who never closed a single day? That's right folks—Retail pharmacies. Big box chains. Always here for your amusement to abuse, to annoy, and to demean. Some of you may be thinking: "Abuse? Annoy? Demean? My pharmacists love me!" No, they don't. I promise, they don't. They are tired of being yelled at and called names every day because someone decided to impose their problems upon everyone else. Your inability to manage time, manage

ROYA JOYA · 111

your own insurance, manage your own kids—these are not my issues.

As corporations tried to come up with their own plans on how to address COVID, there were plenty of people taking advantage of the mass hysteria and resulting situations that presented themselves. Stores were closing due to full staff walk outs after someone coughed in their vicinity. Now imagine, as a healthcare professional, you shut down your pharmacy because a single person coughed in the building. Ah well, we've all taken advantage of freedom at some point. Hell, if I knew I could get away with it, I would do it now just to get a break!

COVID introduced many challenges to the retail world. Supply chain shortages, workforce shortages, careless attitudes. The people the world once referred to as "HEROES" were now "IDIOTS" because they couldn't dispense opioids weeks early. To be clear, there is NO REASON, no pandemic, no natural disaster, no zombie apocalypse that will justify filling narcotics weeks in advance. We are saving you a trip in an ambulance to the morgue—you are very welcome. As time went on, the narrative evolved from "HERO" to "YOU'RE NOT MY DOCTOR." Well, I'd like to begin by saying: Yes, I am not your doctor, and I am very grateful for that fact. However, I still do have to monitor the medications you take and make sure you do not have harmful side effects or reactions (no matter how deserving one may be).

In all of these moments of chaos, vicious anger, and ridiculous tantrums; we stood behind the counter and did our best not to walk into traffic after work.

When the community swarmed the stores and purchased every last item from the shelves (not even leaving snacks for the pharmacy to have during work hours), we considered candy as our new diets.

As customers paid with cash and told us they had COVID seconds before they drove off; we washed our hands, wiped the counter, and prayed for the best.

When shields and masks were only for customer sales and NOT distributed to the medical staff behind the counter, we continued about our days as customers screamed with their Daffy Duck spitfire in our faces.

And when the bargains store quality shields the company gifted us broke after a week, we used cat litter to hold them up and create a boundary that would then be pushed down by every other patient.

Moral of the story? We did it all. Together, we did it all. We survived it all and in worse shape than some of you can imagine. As mental health dwindled and pizza was dangled in front of us as compensation, it became clear that not only the world but the corporations did not understand the decline of its employees and the human race.

I feel like COVID is something we can talk about for an entire book, but it wouldn't do justice to the real-life scenes we witnessed every day. Nothing will baffle me more than society's complete and utter lack of human decency and care. It still amazes me to this day how unwilling people are to help each other. I'm not speaking in regards to fundraisers or community events; I mean everyday stranger-to-stranger interactions.

Cutting an elderly person in the checkout line because they were moving too slow with their walker. Jumping across a counter to grab the last at-home testing kit because your job says they'll fire you if you don't have a test done in forty-eight hours.

Trying to purchase the last ten at-home testing kits because you "have a big family" and you're disregarding the people in line behind you. Holding up the vaccine window because you think you deserve the vaccine appointment you scheduled last week and didn't show up for but have time to get today.

Many of these scenes are burned in our memories as dark days that we can only hope are in the past. These incidents have forced a lot of healthcare professionals to leave the industry and pursue different careers. These attitudes coupled with corporate demand have sparked national outrage and labor shortages. Do not be shocked as our pharmacies close down earlier and open later because there is no one willing to deal with your attitude.

# The Final Chapter

In a world where society is constantly evolving and privilege only continues to grow, I never thought I would see the final chapter. However, this is the final chapter for this journey and those alike. While I move on to the next portion of my professional career, I can't help but to look back on all of the adventures I have endured over the last twelve years. Yep, that's right. It has been twelve whole years in the making. Sure, every word isn't documented, every moment isn't immortalized. Together we laughed, we cried, we vented, and we pushed forward. The patient-facing world will continue to do just that—push forward.

My goal is to provide some stress relief by bringing these stories to life and entertaining my peers. I have spent the last decade of my career trading experiences among colleagues and other professionals only to find that people are crazy everywhere. While this book is brutally honest and solely one person's opinion, I hope that you have found a smile in some form. This book is a way to remind us all that though our careers are serious, it's okay to smile and laugh to get through the terrible times. When the world around you feels like its falling apart, find light in even the darkest place.

# Acknowledgments

I wanted to take a moment and thank everyone who made these stories immortal. While I can't name each and every single person who made an impact on my journey, I wanted to highlight a few.

Sydney, you are the absolute soul behind every comma and period. Thank you for all the time, encouragement, and creativity you have extended. Your enthusiasm to live life motivated me to keep moving forward even if I'm not trotting across the globe. Thank you for always answering the phone to provide continuous reassurance and a bountiful of excitement! You're the best, bestie.

Zack, thank you for being the best support system to every crazy idea I have. You have been nothing less than encouraging, thoughtful, and understanding. Thank you for always helping me laugh through the toughest days!

Thank you to my creativity team- Vanessa for your amazing cover ideas, Ashley for the creative design, and Haley for walking me through the process! Each of you have been an absolute blessing and I appreciate every insight, idea, and suggestion you have provided to get me to this point!

Thank you to my family for indulging in my craziness and allowing me to live out every crazy dream!

And lastly, thank you to every employee, colleague, and teammate that basked in the laughter and decline of humanity.

Manufactured by Amazon.ca
Bolton, ON

26083673R00069